D0667514

12/15

BY
SCOTT SONNEBORN
ILLUSTRATED BY
OMAR LOZANO

CASE 002

Meet the South Police

PICTURE WINDOW BOOKS
A CAPSTONE IMPRINT

WITHDRAWN
FREMONT PUBLIC LIBRARY DISTRICT
1170 N. Midlothian Road
Mundelein, IL 60060

The North Police is published by
Picture Window Books
a Capstone Imprint
1710 Roe Crest Drive
North Mankato, Minnesota 56003
www.capstonepub.com

Copyright © 2016 Scott Sonneborn
No part of this publication may be reproduced in whole or in part,
or stored in a retrieval system, or transmitted in any form or by any
means, electronic, mechanical, photocopying, recording, or otherwise,
without written permission of the publisher.

Cataloging-in-Publication Data is available at the Library of Congress website.
ISBN: 978-1-4795-6486-6 (library binding)
ISBN: 978-1-4747-0031-3 (paperback)
ISBN: 978-1-4747-0036-8 (eBook)

Summary: One of the North Police's two greatest detectives is missing in action! The South Police send their best officer to help crack the case. Unfortunately, the two police stations are polar opposites!

Designer: Bob Lentz

Printed in China by Nordica
0415/CA21500537
042015 008843NORDF15

TABLE OF CONTENTS

CHAPTER 1
Missing! 7

CHAPTER 2
Honk! 13

CHAPTER 3
Rescue! 19

(NORTH POHL-eess)

The North Police are

the elves who solve crimes

at the North Pole.

These are their stories . . .

CHAPTER 1

Missing!

Detective Sprinkles of the North Police rushed into the chief's office.

"Detective Sugarplum is gone, sir," cried Sprinkles. "She's been missing all day!"

"That's because she's on vacation," replied the chief.

It was the day after Christmas. After working so hard on December 25, many elves had taken the day off.

"But what if there's trouble?" Sprinkles worried. "I've never solved a case without a partner."

"You won't have to," said the chief.

"The South Police sent one of their best officers to fill in," the chief explained.

The South Police officer waddled into the room.

"HONK!" he said.

Sprinkles leaned over to the chief. "Sir, that's a penguin," he whispered.

"Of course," said the chief. "That's who lives in the South Pole!"

"All the best officers in the South Police are penguins," the chief added.

"HONK!" agreed the penguin.

Suddenly, the police radio on the chief's desk squawked.

"There's trouble on the Christmas Town highway!" said a voice over the radio.

CHAPTER 2

Honk!

The Christmas Town highway was jammed with elves returning to the North Pole after their day off.

The tow sleigh couldn't get through to the trouble.

"No problem," said Sprinkles. "I'll just use my sleigh bell siren."

Sprinkles hit the button.

Nothing happened.

The sleigh bell siren was broken!

"Oh, no!" said Sprinkles. "How will we get through all this traffic?"

"HONK!" said the penguin.

"Great idea!" said Detective Sprinkles.

Sprinkles honked the police sleigh's horn.

BEEP-BEEP! The traffic moved out of the way.

Sprinkles and the South Police officer led the tow sleigh to the trouble.

It was Sugarplum! The ice road had cracked under her sleigh. She was stuck!

Suddenly, the ice broke! Sugarplum's sleigh fell toward the icy water below.

"Oh, no!" cried Sprinkles. "If she hits the water, she'll be frozen for sure!"

CHAPTER 3

Rescue!

Detective Sprinkles jumped onto the tow sleigh. He grabbed the tow rope. Sprinkles threw the rope to Sugarplum as she fell.

But he missed!

"HONK!" cried the South Police Officer.

The penguin dove through the air. He grabbed the rope in his beak.

The penguin hooked the rope onto Sugarplum's sleigh as it dropped through the air.

Then the South Police Officer splashed down into the freezing water!

The rope caught the sleigh just in time. Detective Sugarplum was safe!

But what about the South Police Officer?

"HONK!" said the penguin as he popped out of the water. He was okay, too!

"That water is much too cold for an elf," said Detective Sprinkles.

"But for a penguin," Sprinkles added, "I guess the water is just right."

The tow sleigh pulled Sugarplum and her sleigh back onto the road.

"I knew you'd get here in time, Detective Sprinkles," Sugarplum said. "The North Police are always there when you need them."

"So are the South Police," added Sprinkles.

"HONK!" agreed the penguin.

The North Police smiled.

"Another case neatly wrapped!" they cheered.

CASE SAVED!

6' 6"

6' 0"

5' 6"

5' 0"

4' 6"

4' 0"

3' 6"

3' 0"

CASE 002 NORTH POLICE

SOUTH POLICE

Penguin • Height 3'0" • Weight 50

GLOSSARY

detective (di-TEK-tiv) — one who investigates crimes

partner (PART-nuhr) — one of two people who do something together

siren (SYE-ruhn) — a device that makes a loud sound, which is used as a warning

sleigh (SLAY) — a sled usually pulled by horses or other animals

waddled (WAHD-uhld) — walked strangely, taking short steps and swaying from side to side

THE
NORTH
POLICE

These are their stories . . .

only from

PICTURE WINDOW BOOKS!

AUTHOR

Scott Sonneborn has written dozens of books, one circus (for Ringling Bros. Barnum & Bailey), and a bunch of TV shows. He's been nominated for one Emmy and spent three very cool years working at DC Comics. He lives in Los Angeles with his wife and their two sons.

ILLUSTRATOR

Omar Lozano lives in Monterrey, Mexico. He has always been crazy for illustration, constantly on the lookout for awesome things to draw. In his free time, he watches lots of movies, reads fantasy and sci-fi books, and draws! Omar has worked for Marvel, DC, IDW, Capstone, and more.